UNSEEMLY

JASON PARENT

UNSEEMLY
Copyright © 2016 by Jason Parent
All rights reserved.

FIRST EDITION

January 2016

ISBN-10: 1523980303
ISBN-13: 978-1523980307

This book is a work of fiction. Names, characters, places, and incidents are either a product of the author's imagination or are used fictitiously, unless explicit permission was granted for use. Any resemblance to actual events, locales, or persons, living or dead, is entirely coincidental. This book or portions thereof may not be reproduced in any form without the express written permission of the publisher. The author assumes responsibility for the content of his work.

Cover Illustration by Tenebrae Studios.

UNSEEMLY

PETER CALLUM STARED at the behemoth with the slack jaw and handlebar mustache, slouching in a corner booth and guzzling down what Peter guessed to be his sixth or seventh beer. He wondered, and not for the first time, why in the sake of all that was good and holy and contrary to that hateful man had he come to Scotland.

It came down to a nose, he figured. Dervish could sniff out means to acquire surplus income: blood money, the kind that couldn't be cleaned no matter how many times you laundered it. And he didn't care who he had to lie, cheat, or steal from to get it.

Despite traveling two thousand miles through bumpy air and bumpier water, the man who had summoned him there a mere ten meters away, Peter still thought his best bet was to just turn around and pretend he'd never heard the invitation left on his voicemail.

If I had any brains, that's exactly what I'd do. He ran a hand through his shaggy brown hair, thick with salt, before glancing around the tavern for a captain of any of the rot-wood dinghies he'd seen dumped lazily upon the shore. He'd have settled for a paddleboat, anyway off that inbred-infested shit heap of an island. Fifteen minutes on that speck of dirt too many kilometers off the coast to swim had been fifteen minutes too long.

Dungarradh, he scoffed and scratched the nape of his neck. The itch persisted. So did Peter's scratching, until he broke open the bug-bitten skin. *They ought to call it Midge-Infested Shithole.*

As if on cue, something itched beneath his worn jeans. He let out a low growl and slapped his thigh until the sting went numb.

An old man smoking a thick stogie chortled out gray clouds. He leaned forward on an antique loveseat, ash falling off the cigar onto velvet cushions and the hardwood floor. "You best be keeping away from some bits o' the beach," he said, his face red with drink. His laughter brought on a coughing fit, and he spit green phlegm into a handkerchief. His voice lowered, and his expression soured. "Nasty wee beasties... They'll get you if you're no' careful."

The man went quiet. He stared with milky, cataract-covered eyes that bore straight into Peter's soul. It made his skin crawl.

The man burst out into a bellowing laugh. He laughed so hard he farted. "I'm just pulling your tit, lad."

Peter released his breath. *That's it.* He set his jaw and resolved to be on the first boat back to the mainland.

"Ignore him," a gorgeous brunette said as she slid a finger down his shoulder. She looked to be in her mid-twenties with curves in all the right places and a girl-next-door face that hinted something devilish in the corners.

She pointed into the pub. "I think your friends are over there. The big one asked me to come fetch you."

Peter's eyes were slow to follow. He traced the length of a sculpted bicep, down a creamy-smooth forearm, to the long, lithe finger tipped in blood-red nail polish. As his gaze left the finger, it landed on Dervish, and their eyes met. A smile crept across the barbarian's round face, crinkling his mustache into boomerangs.

"Fuck," Peter muttered. *Can't leave now. He's seen me. Do I really need the money this badly?* But he knew that he did. He owed money everywhere: the bank for the mortgage on a house his ex-wife lived in with her new lover, Steve; the child support payments (for two kids that looked nothing like him) that always seemed due the second he scrounged up enough money to pay off the prior one; the piece of shit Hyundai he had to get to replace the BMW Steve now drove; and the more than frequent drinking and whoring and the occasional snort of coke he needed to get him through the lonely hours of night.

Despite all his vices, and he readily conceded there were many, Peter was no deadbeat. But going legit, conducting *real* archeology, didn't pay his kind of bills unless he made that one remarkable find. The tibia of a Druid and a mummified dog didn't have much resale value. He needed his Dead Sea Scrolls or

Rosetta Stone.

Failure made his saliva taste bitter. He'd promised himself no more grave robbing, no more wild goose chases, no more Dervish. But his wife had absconded with eighty percent of what was supposed to be a hidden cache of untaxed income, Maria justifying an equal split plus fifteen percent for each kid and promising to go to the cops if he uttered even the slightest protest. Peter walked away from his sedentary life with less than two hundred thousand of his hard-earned, albeit ill-begotten, gains.

I should have let the bitch go to the cops and watched her hang alongside me for tax evasion. Peter huffed and cloaked his loathing with a smile as phony as a five-dollar palm reader. Straightening, he made his way to the corner booth. His money long gone, bills to pay, Peter knew he was going to break his promise.

Here I am again. Grave robbing.

"Peter!" Dervish shouted cheerfully as though he were greeting an old friend, a point with which Peter would have contended. He likened the brute to dead insects in a pool; he always surfaced sooner or later, and when he did, Peter's whole environment was corrupted.

Dervish waved an arm, ushering Peter to the empty spot on his left. "Sit! Sit!"

"Dervish." Peter nodded curtly. He unzipped his leather jacket, hung it on the pole beside the booth, and plopped into the seat.

A rather curious gentleman sat to Dervish's right. He was garbed in a plain gray fedora and a tweed jacket, the kind with the brown patches on the elbow. He didn't fit the profile of Dervish's usual sorts, a scholar who'd probably never hit a weight room in his life. Bifocals hung at the end of a long, narrow nose, bony and edgy like the rest of the gaunt, slender man's features. As if afraid to make eye contact, he studied the glass of soda in front of him, slurping the dark brown liquid through a straw.

Peter didn't know what to make of the fellow. His curiosity was momentarily abated, his eyes averting as Dervish leaned in close. Wrists too thick to wear a watch slid across the table, making Peter's own wrists look feeble. Those meaty paws were clasped white-knuckle tight as if their owner was trying to restrain them. Dervish's hot breath reeked of beer. Peter saw wildness in the man's deep brown eyes, a peculiar light dancing across his irises, a hint of frenzy the likes of which Peter hadn't seen for nearly a decade.

But he remembered it.

It was a look that usually landed one or more of their brood in some foreign prison, way up shit's proverbial creek, or worse, counting grains of dirt for all eternity. Peter swallowed hard as the thought crossed his mind that this time, it could be him.

Dervish's excitement waned, and he appeared lost in thought. At last, he whispered, "I've found them, Peter." Only the gleam on his incisors could rival that returning to his eyes. The man was damn near salivating. "Right here. On this island."

Peter sighed. He knew he was going to regret his next question, the answer to which would explain Dervish's insistence that Peter fly out on a moment's notice and his promise of a potentially massive payroll. "Found what?"

"Not what, Peter. Who. The *sidhe*."

"She? She who?"

"No, you know, the *daoinesith*?"

Peter squinted, rummaging through his brain for words vaguely familiar but perhaps long forgotten. He came up short, while the makings of a nursery rhyme lingered beyond the tip of his tongue.

Dervish persisted. "The bloody fae, mate."

"Fae?"

"Oh, now you're just being daft. Kelpies, selkies, naiad, spriggans…don't make me say it. It sounds so much worse than it is if you make me say it."

Peter shook his head. "Are you speaking gibberish? Is this some kind of a joke?" His eyes shifted to the man at Dervish's right, who offered no comment, then back to Dervish.

"The goddamn faeries!" Dervish shouted, loud enough to be heard over the Celtic fiddle. A few folks looked their way. Dervish grinned. "My friend here just came out of the closet." The patrons paid them no further mind, except a stylish gent who gave Peter a long once-over.

"You're joking?" Peter laughed. Dervish did not. "Wait. You mean you're serious?" He launched to his feet and slammed his palms into the table. The pint glasses rattled. "You had me fly all the way out to Glasgow, hire a boat to take me to this insignificant dirt mound no one else has even heard of, where sand fleas have taken up a fucking summer home in my pubic hair and are biting like starved piranha, all for some ridiculous…"

Peter clenched his fists and his teeth, trying to stop them both from lashing out. He scratched his leg, the reminder of the bites making him itch. He sneered. "For some stupid fucking old wives' tale? The Holy Grail? El Dorado? The Fountain of Youth? You're a fucking asshole, Dervish. You always were, and you always will be." He turned and grabbed his jacket.

"Shhh!" Dervish grabbed his sleeve. He smiled. "What in God's name is a sand flea? I think maybe you brought those with you, mate."

"Take your fucking hand off me."

"Just sit your ass down and hear me out."

His former partner in crime was still smiling, which only made Peter hotter. He tore his arm free and threw on his coat.

The man in the fedora looked up from his drink, a callous flat line where his lips met. "Please, Mr. Callum. Sit down."

Peter paused. The serene yet grave tone of the man's voice gave him an air of authority that belied his timid appearance. Hesitantly, Peter sat, almost as if the man had willed him back into the booth with some trick of the mind.

"I am Liam McCoy," he said in a heavy Irish brogue. "I am a professor of classical literature at a university near Dublin. I enjoy what I do, but my real passion, and the focus of many years of study, lies in tracing the lineage of folklore and legends back to their origins, to give reasons to the words, motives to the morality tales. Many of the world's most well-known and oft-mistold allegories were conceived long before the written word, passed down by generation after generation through psalms, fables, and lullabies."

Peter rolled his eyes. "Don't tell me you buy into

his nonsense, Professor." He hooked a finger at Dervish who bounced in his seat, giddy as a child on Christmas morning. "Look, I've been down that road. I've known this bastard for a long time. Believe me when I say that listening to his lies may make you slightly richer, but it's a heck of a lot more likely to get you killed."

"And yet, you're here." The professor folded his hands together. "I share your skepticism with respect to the existence of..." McCoy grimaced, "faery folk, but tales such as these usually bear some truth... if you know how to find it and are willing to dig deep enough. I am after that truth."

"What truth do you hope to find, Professor?" Peter asked."I guarantee you: you won't find it here."

He pulled a small black book from an inner jacket pocket. "The *daoinesith* are of particular interest to me. Translated from Scottish Gaelic, *daoinesith* means 'people of the mounds.' No doubt you've seen the multitude of sand dunes outside. I assure you, they cover most of the island—more bumps than a teenagers face, I say." At that, the Irishman chuckled. Until then, Peter had thought him humorless, though the joke did little to assure him otherwise.

"Anyway, some of the legends suggest that this *race*, if you'll permit my use of the term, lived in earthen green mounds, which I imagine would not be unlike those sand dunes out there if they were covered in grass. It's not hard to imagine a time centuries ago when they might have been."

Professor McCoy wet his lips. "As far as the tales go, the *daoinesith* occasionally interacted with humans. These interactions were... sometimes good, sometimes not so good. Mostly pranks, relatively harmless stuff. Then there are those few, darker faery tales that talk of kidnappings and murder." He stared at Peter as though assessing him. "I don't suppose you've heard the tale about the smith and the fae?"

Peter shook his head. Although he didn't believe a word of what he was hearing, he had to admit he was fairly interested.

"No? Of course not. Why would you have, being an American and such? My point is...er, where was I?" Professor McCoy cleared his throat. He took another sip of his coke. "No matter. With, er, Mr.? Eh, with *Dervish's* help, I've managed the find versions of several tales that date back to before the spread of Christianity to the British Isles. And I'm sure you can guess where they are most prevalent. Right here in western Scotland and its outlying islands."

"So?" Peter didn't see how tall tales made for fat wallets.

"So, Mr. Callum, I believe that the inhabitants of this village are likely descendants of the people of the mounds—no, not faeries, but perhaps a tribe of humans who believed in the mystic arts. Not so far-fetched really, when you consider Celtic lore."

Peter leaned back against the booth. "Humph. Now there's a theory I might be able to believe. For the sake of argument, let's say I do. Where's the money it?"

"Surely, authentic ninth-century Pict or Gael artifacts must hold some weight for their discoverer in the archeological field? At the very least, the local museums would pay a nice sum for a piece of their heritage. I'm betting those mounds hold a few secrets just waiting to be unearthed by an entrepreneurial sort such as yourself."

Yep. Grave robbing.

"Look around you." Professor McCoy leaned forward and lowered his voice. "This pub is as modern and lavish as any I've come across on the mainland. The locals are dressed in top brand names. Their houses are far from quaint and simple. They don't farm. Aside from a small corner store, a gift shop lining the main street, and the bait and tackle store and boat mechanic down by the docks, I haven't seen any businesses, no other means to make a living whatsoever."

"Except this place."

"Yes, this establishment and the adjacent inn seem to be the only bustling places in town. Everything they have is imported. Their fresh goods come in on a ferry each morning. Living here must cost a fortune. And for what? All that's here is a few kilometers of sand dunes, uncultivated land with a small yet lavish village snuggled at its center. These people have no discernable exports, no identifiable income, yet they don't seem to want for anything."

Peter scanned the interior of the pub and, for the first time, noticed the fine, ornately crafted Scottish oak furniture. The gold-plated chandelier gracing the ceiling illuminated the room through cut glass that sparkled like diamonds. The massive bar lined with top-shelf liquor from around the globe; the fine art where portraits of famous footballers should have been; the elaborate moldings, the antique everythings, and the intricate doilies and fine china; the orchids and lilacs and assortments of other flowers that grew in faraway places, thriving in what looked like Ming Dynasty vases—those, Peter hoped were replicas—the supposedly old English-style tavern was both gaudy and worldly beyond anything he'd expected to find in a largely unknown island town sheltered from the city and its culture.

He glanced at the bartender and gaped when he noticed what ostensibly appeared to be a Rolex on his wrist. Peter hoped that was a fake, too. He also noticed how quickly the bartender looked away and pretended to clean a glass when their eyes met. *Was he watching me?*

Peter squinted at the waitstaff in the bar area. *Who else is watching?* The thought made his collar feel tight, the air a little thicker, and that dull murmur of voices in the background seem unfriendly, suspicious. He turned swiftly in his seat and scanned the tavern. Locals sipped their drinks and watched football or muttered in a dialect Peter's ears weren't equipped to decipher. The sing-song way of their speech was what separated them from tourists, though he didn't think he saw any other tourists. Gentlemen dressed in tailored suits or lounged in sport jackets and loafers. Women donned the latest fashions, with styled hair and lots of precious metal ornamentation. They looked ready for a fancy evening soiree rather than a night out at the pub. The locals might have passed for tourists who didn't know any better had their haughty tones and the way they carried themselves–stiff and standoffish, like they and only they belonged there—revealed their true natures.

As soon as he turned back to Professor McCoy, he could feel the townsfolk's glares like shadows hovering over his shoulder. A chill ran through his bones. McCoy grimaced and nodded as if he had felt it too.

"A round of drinks," a comely barmaid announced, startling Peter from his deliberation. "On the house." The tall, wavy haired brunette in her mid-twenties smiled at Peter as she deposited three pints on the tabletop. She leaned across the table to slide a glass to Dervish, a considerable amount of cleavage spilling out of her low-cut top as she did. Peter took a large gulp of ice-cold beer, all the while staring over the lip of his glass to take in the free peep show. But as she retreated, she caught him ogling. He could feel the heat of embarrassment flush through his cheeks.

The barmaid winked and smiled as she strutted away. Peter liked that view just as well.

Dervish nudged him in the arm, pointing out what Peter couldn't possibly have missed even if he'd been a hundred years old and cursed with cataracts. The professor straightened his fedora and seemed not to have noticed the buxom beauty.

He's come to see the faeries, Peter sniggered.

As he swilled his beer, his uneasiness didn't exactly alleviate, but its edge dulled. "Maybe this is a bustling fishing community," he said to no one in particular.

The pint in front of the professor remained untouched. He passed it to Dervish, who scoffed it up eagerly. McCoy leveled his gaze at Peter. "I have walked the length of this island in half a day's span. I haven't seen a single trawler, no seiners or line vessels, no fishing boats of any kind, at least none large enough for commercial fishing, nor have I seen any piers large enough or deep enough to dock one.

"Old money—"

"From where? Do these people look like royalty, or oil barons, or technological whiz kids, like your Bill Gates? No, they are simpler folk disguised in the trappings of the wealthy. I doubt they have any knowledge or care for what goes on beyond the confines of their little island, save for the football match and how to spend their money."

Peter was starting to put two and two together. There was more to the legends than just faeries. He turned to his former business partner. Dervish had knocked back his beer and most of the professor's. "You're crazy, that's for sure, but you've never been stupid. You can't tell me you honestly believe these people are waist deep in... what exactly? Faery gold?"

Dervish chugged the rest of his beer. Froth fizzled on his mustache, and he wiped his mouth with his sleeve. "Treasure? I'm open to the possibility and, fuck yeah, I'll take it if we find it. But that's not what I'm here for, mate. Nope, my benefactor has plenty of that already. He's after something far more valuable to him, and he's willing to pay me handsomely for it."

Peter raised an eyebrow. "How handsomely?"

"Five hundred thousand euros. Clean money, not the kind we're used to, huh old friend?" He swatted Peter on the arm. "The way I figure it, we'll split it five ways. That's a nice chunk of change each for a night's work, I'd say. Mostly legal, too, I think. And if we find anything else of value, we'll split that evenly, too."

Peter donned his see-through smile. He knew

Dervish well enough to know that when he was *saying* five hundred thousand, he was *getting* at least a million, maybe a lot more. "I want two hundred."

The professor looked up. He sucked air through his straw. Dervish's grin finally faltered. "We can talk about that later."

"And you said 'five ways.' I only see me, you, and the fedora over here."

"Well there's Corbin—"

"Not that asshole." Peter hung his head and released a sigh. "Where is that old son of a bitch?"

"He's watching over our things. Just a precaution. I haven't seen a damn thing here yet I couldn't handle by my lonesome. I'm beginning to wonder why I invited the lot of you, but now that you're all here... Anyway, we have all the things you said you'd need for a proper dig. I doubt we're going to need any of it."

"Oh yeah? Why's that?"

That gleam in Dervish's eyes burned like fire. "'Cause we found them, Pete. We've actually found them, hiding here in plain sight!"

Peter crossed his arms. "You've seen them then? With your own two eyes?"

"Well, no... not exactly."

"I don't know why I ever agreed to entertain your bullshit. Man, I should have known better. I swear to God, Dervish—"

Dervish slumped forward. "Matt saw them."

"Matt's here? You brought your boy into this line of work?" Peter rubbed his forehead. The last time he'd seen Matt, the boy was still in secondary. He'd been a tall reed, not quite a man, with an innocent smile and shy manner and none of his father's vices. He'd taken a shining to the boy, considered him family even. He guessed that the apple drank from the same water as the poisoned tree no matter how early and far away it might fall.

"He hasn't been a boy for several years now." Dervish straightened and raised his chin. "He's probably got more hair on his chest and fillies under his belt than you do."

Peter frowned. "He was such a great kid. Must you corrupt everything you touch?"

"Hey!" Dervish shouted, throwing his hands up. "He wanted to come. Practically begged me. He was excited to do it, *and* he was excited to see you."

"Don't make this my fault."

"I'm not. Who else could I trust to go on ahead? Corbin? You and I both know he'd try to steal all the gold and glory for himself. You? I had to use all the guile I had in me just to lure you out of your sedentary lifestyle. Damn it, mate. You're like an old bloke. No offense, Professor."

"None taken."

"Anyway," Dervish continued, "the boy's green, I'll give you that. But he's ambitious, eager to please, and above all, loyal. Besides, this was supposed to be easy-peasy, a recon mission to scope out a remote beach. How was I supposed to know he'd actually find something?"

"So where is he?" Peter asked. "I want to hear it from the horse's mouth."

Dervish slumped forward again. His chin dropped. "Not sure. I gave him a two-day head start, you know, to do some light surveillance while Corbin and I gathered anything we might need for an excavation. After the flight into Glasgow, I met with an associate to procure some added protection." He patted his chest to where Peter knew a pistol was hiding under his jacket. "I have an extra piece for you, if you want it."

"If you remember, I nearly blew my goddamn foot off the last time I handled one of those things."

Dervish roared with laughter. "Fucking Calcutta. What a mess that was. I'd drink to good times, but it appears I'm all out of drink."

"Can we get back to Matt?" The last thing Peter wanted to think about was Calcutta and was already sorry he'd brought it up. That "mess" Dervish found so riotously funny left one of their team dead, another missing and long-since presumed dead, and poor Peter minus a toe. It was one of the many reasons he decided the straight life was for the better.

"Matt's, uh, not answering his phone."

"What?" Peter rose. A sudden urge to run for the hills came over him, and he almost did. But on an island as small as Dungarradh, there's nowhere to run.

"Oh will you relax? Did that ex-wife of yours take your balls too in the divorce? It's only been a day, and the boy drinks and fucks like his pop. He left me a message last night. Here." Dervish pulled a cell phone from his pocket. "You'll want to hear it for yourself, I suppose."

Dervish hit some buttons and handed the phone over. Peter read Matt's name on the screen and pushed play on the triangular icon beneath it.

"Dad!" Matt's voice came in with crystal clarity. It

was hushed but excited. Peter heard rumbling in the background. It grew louder and ended with a crash, only to repeat anew. *Waves?*

"I met a girl! She's a barmaid at the pub. She's so fine... you have to meet her. I started chatting her up at the bar, and, well, one thing led to another. I think I'm in love. Anyway, we're at the beach beyond the thickets. You'll know the place when you get here. I have to hurry. She thinks I'm taking a piss, and I promised I wouldn't tell anyone about this place. Dad..." Matt took a deep, audible breath. "They're real! They're really fucking real!"

A woman called to Matt, her voice faint. Not all the words were clear, but they were spoken in that sing-song Scottish way. Peter thought she might have actually been singing.

"I have to go," Matt said. "Get here as soon as you can. I'm moving in for a closer look now. I'll take a video and send it to you, if I can do it without her noticing. Don't want to mess things up. I think she might love me too, Dad. Gotta go!"

The call cut off. "Where's the video?" Peter asked.

Dervish retrieved his phone. "He didn't send one."

"Well, where the fuck is he?"

"What can I say? The boy's a romantic. He was probably drinking and shagging that floozy 'til the wee hours of the morning and is now sleeping it off somewhere."

Peter noticed Dervish's usual carefree bravado was absent from his voice. He was about to comment when the professor spoke first.

"As I mentioned, I have already visited the bulk

of the island. Whatever lies beyond those thickets that Matt was talking about is the only place I've yet to explore. By land, there appears to be only one way in, a narrow pathway through what might as well be a field of barbed wire, brush so thick with thorns and broken twigs that it's simply impassable. A padlocked wooden gate blocks the path itself, but I was able to see beyond it by peeking through the slats. Not that there was much to see. Just a tunnel shrouded in darkness, leading down and reeking of brine. I can't be certain, but if I had to guess, it'll lead us to where Matt was last night."

"So that's our entry point?" Peter asked, realizing too late that he might have just committed himself to the expedition, at least in Dervish's eyes.

The reemergence of the criminal's smug grin all but confirmed it. "Unless you got a boat?"

"I hired a local to bring me out here, same as you, I'm guessing. It was hard enough trying to find a captain who'd come near this place. 'Bad luck,' they said. I'm beginning to see why."

Dervish nodded. McCoy, who hadn't drunk a sip of alcohol as far as Peter could tell, signaled the barmaid for the bill.

Peter sighed. "When do we do it?"

"Tonight. Matt's call came just after three o'clock. If that's when he saw them, that's when we'll be there. We'll meet outside around the corner of the hotel in the service alley at quarter of. "He tossed a card key onto the table. "I got you a room. Rest up, get some grub, explore the island. Just be ready to go when it's time."

He stood. His hulking frame towered over the

booth. Peter had forgotten just how big he was, big enough to take on a grizzly and scarred enough to suggest he already had. Dervish was tough as jerky but more flippant than a light switch. The chance to rid himself of debt had driven Peter to that island. Worry for Matt's welfare and the fear of saying no to Dervish would keep him there.

There's no such thing as faeries. Matt was probably smoking some local herb laced with God knows what. Rational thought would not subdue the sense of dread building inside him.

I hope he's okay. He sighed. *Where the hell are you, Matt?*

Momentarily lost in thought, Peter jumped when Dervish's meaty hand grabbed his shoulder. "Slide out. I need to take a piss."

Peter scooted out of the seat. Dervish headed off in search of a restroom.

"He's worried about his son," the professor said, breaking the awkward silence that had followed Dervish's departure. "I think you should take that handgun he offered."

"What about you? You don't look like you're packing."

"Me? I'm afraid I wouldn't know how to handle a gun, much less have the chutzpah to pull a trigger." McCoy laughed nervously. "Oh no. I abhor violence. I won't be much use in a fight if—how do you Americans say it? The shit hits the fan?"

"Good to know. But if you suspect trouble, what are you doing here?"

"I'm a scholar, Mr. Callum. This will not be the first time my curiosity gets me into trouble."

Peter scoffed. "Just hope it's not the last."

When Dervish returned, the barmaid had not yet brought their check. He slapped fifty pounds on the table and said, "I'm heading to my room. You boys are welcome to stay here as long as you like, but remember what I said: we go at three."

Professor McCoy stood. "I think I will take my leave as well. Thank you for the drinks." He tipped his cap at Peter. "Mr. Callum."

Peter rose and followed the others through the tavern and into the hotel lobby. As he crossed the threshold, a boy not more than twelve years-old wearing a North Face fleece and a pair of untied Nike's butted him with his shoulder. Peter's hand instinctively checked for his wallet. He found it in his back pocket where it belonged.

The boy glared at him, something akin to malice in his eyes. He rounded a corner and was gone, leaving Peter to wonder what he had missed.

Back in his room, Peter decided to get some rest before the planned late-night activities. Before lying down, he emptied his pockets. In his jacket, he found a small, folded square of paper. The note jotted on it said: *Leave. It's not safe here for you.*

The warning was far from subtle. Peter was of a mind to heed it. But when he thought back to the last time he'd seen Matt, a kid then about the same age as his son now, he couldn't abandon the boy to his father's transgressions. He lay down on his bed and closed his eyes, wondering what sort of trouble awaited him.

Idiots, all of them, he thought as he drifted toward sleep. *There's no such fucking thing as fucking faeries.*

***

PETER AWOKE to a knock at his door.

"Mr. Callum," the shrill voice of the professor said as it passed through the solid wood. "It's time."

Peter plucked a crustie from the corner of his eye and kicked his legs over the side of the bed. Still fully clothed and feeling a little jet lagged, he walked to the door, wishing someone had brewed a pot of coffee. He yawned as he reached for the knob.

When he opened the door, Professor McCoy paced on the other side, his face pale, wrought with worry. Darkened flesh circled his eyes, making them appear as though they had receded into their sockets. He was wearing the same clothes he'd been wearing earlier, only now they were considerably more wrinkled. Even his fedora looked as though he'd slept on it.

"Are you ready to go?" he asked between bites on his thumbnail.

"As ready as I'm going to be." Peter pulled a black hoodie from his suitcase and threw it on. He glanced at his watch: 2:47 am. He couldn't decide if it was too fucking late or too goddamn early, his days of pulling late-nighters a thing of the past. Either way, he was starting to miss his small apartment back in Columbus, where faeries only existed in children's books and Disney cartoons, not in the minds of grown men.

Stepping lightly, he followed the professor down a stairwell and through the exit at the bottom. The gravel road in front of the inn had no streetlights. But the gray globe face of a fat moon cast everything in a silvery shimmer. Peter and McCoy hugged close to the building as they made their way around it to the service alley, trying to keep to the shadows but finding none to keep to. Staying hidden seemed pointless anyway. The town was asleep with all the folks in it.

Except those stupid enough to be chasing silly fantasies.

They turned into the alley shaded by the building, where glowing yellow-green eyes met them. They seemed to float in the darkness. Peter took a hesitant step forward. The eyes leaped from an unseen perch and, at knee level, came toward him fast. Peter stood his ground. The thing to which the eyes belonged kept charging.

It came into the light and collided with his shin. A black cat rubbed its cheek against him, kissing Peter's legs as it made figure eights around them. Professor McCoy smiled. They both crouched to pet the docile creature.

"What's your name?" Peter asked. He checked for tags but found none. An old wound humped its skin where a patch of hair was missing from its side. The cat looked like it had been stabbed with a twenty-gauge needle.

Peter instantly fell in love with the creature. "A black cat on such a magical night? You must be a Merlin. Yeah, you look like a Merlin to me." He rubbed under the cat's chin. Its eyes closed, and it began to purr.

McCoy sneezed. He backed away. "I shouldn't have done that." His voice sounded as if he had suddenly come down with a cold. "I like cats, but I'm allergic."

They waited in silence, the night quiet except for the sound of the surf in the distance and the soft purrs of their feline friend. At 3:12 am, Dervish entered the alley with Corbin in tow. Each carried what looked like a large oblong tote or suitcase. On closer inspection, Dervish's wasn't a bag at all but a crate large enough to fit a collie. In his other hand, an animal harness, the pole-with-the-circular-cable kind Peter had seen animal control officers on TV use to noose stray dogs and the occasional raccoon.

The crazy bastard really thinks he's going to snag a faery. Peter wondered if faeries even had necks.

Corbin, a stout man with a long pony tail despite only half a head of hair and an evil eye scarred white by one of many deals gone bad, lugged a giant duffel bag into the alley. He dropped it at Peter's feet, its contents clanging, breaking the silence with a metallic cacophony.

Peter winced. Dervish shook his head. Corbin just shrugged. An unlit cigarette dangled from his lower lip. He crouched, unzipped the bag, and pulled out a shovel, which he thrust into Peter's hand.

"What's this for?" Peter asked. "I thought we didn't need to dig?"

Corbin smirked. "Insurance. I've got mine right here." He drew a revolver that had been tucked into the back of his pants and patted it. Peter wondered if it was the same gun Dervish had offered him. *Nah. Corbin is too wild for a gun. Even Dervish knows better than to give him one.* But when he saw the lack of surprise in the big oaf's face, he wasn't so sure.

"Besides," he said, tucking the gun back into his pants, "I was sick of carrying it."

Merlin rubbed against Corbin's leg, and he kicked the poor animal. The cat ran off.

Peter started to protest when Corbin lit the cigarette that had been hanging from his mouth and offered it to him. He declined.

"Suit yourself. How you been, mother fucker? Been a long time."

Not long enough. "It sure has."

"You still chasing tail?"

"I'm married… was married." Peter twirled the wedding band still on his finger. He'd grown so accustomed to it being there that not wearing it felt like a part of him was missing. He sighed. *She probably took that part in the divorce.*

"Oh, yeah. Sorry, man." Corbin stared blankly. His dead eye didn't look sorry. "Dervish had said something about that."

"Yeah," Dervish said. "I told you not to mention it."

Corbin took a long drag on his cigarette, then blew out a cloud of smoke. "Was she fat?"

"All right," Dervish said. He drew the group, all dressed in black tops and dark jeans except the professor, into a huddle. "Enough catching up. You two can make out all you want later. For now, pull up your tights, and let's get moving." He nodded at Professor McCoy, who trotted to the end of the alley, looked both ways down the street, and beckoned the group to follow. He ran to the far side of the gravel road lined with houses spaced few and far between and huge front lawns lacking any tree cover.

Dervish ran to catch up. Peter waved his arm and bowed slightly. "After you."

Corbin winked and made an annoying clicking sound with his mouth. He tossed the duffel bag over his shoulder and jogged after the others. The sound of the tools jingling in the bag lessened as the distance between them grew.

A soft meow came from Peter's left. Merlin swaggered back into the alley and gave him a kiss. "Well, Merlin, if I am going to back out, I suppose now's the time." He squatted, careful not to scare the cat as he lowered the shovel, and stroked Merlin behind its ears. The feline purred like a Harley. Peter stood. "It was a pleasure to meet you, friend."

He ran after the others. Merlin followed.

The four men and one cat walked briskly in a single file line. Once they were out of the town's center, residences were rare. The road became a dirt path. The grass beside it became sand. The sand piled into dunes that rolled out to an ocean they could hear but couldn't see. Acre upon acre of sand dunes rose like mounds of dirt piled beside open graves. A rotted fence—really just crooked wooden spikes about a meter apart and occasionally bound together with kinked and rusting steel wire—began somewhere past the last house Peter had seen. A few weeds lined several of the posts, the only vegetation, the only sign of life, Peter could see.

The night was silent, so they were too. He saw no one on the road and no one off it. The only sounds came from the fall of their footsteps, the light jingle of Corbin's bag, the creak of Dervish's cage, and the purr of their tagalong.

After another kilometer, the path thinned, sand encroaching on both sides. The ocean loomed in every direction somewhere in the distance, but closer now than it had been since his arrival. Peter could smell and taste it on the air.

As they walked, mountainous dunes slowly shrank to mole hills. Just beyond rose a graveyard of thorn bushes and fallen branches from trees that didn't exist. It covered the landscape, looking as though it ranged all the way to Dungarradh's edge. The entire island seemed to have been stripped of its lumber, its trees gnarled and splintered by some wicked mangler machine and thrown into blackthorns and thistles to form a massive spread of thorny vines and jagged roots in that one location, a sort of dead plant dumping ground. Twig spears, roughly hewn and knobbed like the fingers of old men, filled the gaps in what appeared to be a naturally occurring thicket made unnatural by what was tossed there and left to die. The effect of the transplanted wood was to transform an already dangerous copse into a nightmarish barricade that would prove a lesson in excised flesh to anyone who tried to cross it. And in it, dark and deep, only wicked things stirred.

Peter heard the roaring waves, now much louder and closer than they'd been at the start of their excursion. He smelled the acrid stench of seaweed, like boiled dinner left sitting on a stovetop for a month. He licked his lips and tasted salt. But he could not see the water. The league of treacherous dead florae between him and it was tall put not tall enough to prevent his view beyond to where he thought sky met terra not-so-firma. He should have been able to see the swells but could only make out dark sky made darker by the absence of stars the lower his gaze went. Somehow, the horizon escaped the eerie, fish-scale glow of the moon.

They pressed on a short distance and reached the gate that Professor McCoy had told Peter about. The professor was studying the padlock that he'd said had barred the door, only now it was open. He peeked through the slats, then pressed his ear to the fence. "I don't hear anything. I can't see in there beyond a meter or two. Too dark."

Dervish placed a finger over his lips. He pushed past the professor, creaked open the door, and peeked inside. "I can't see shit." He opened the door wider and stepped under the cover of thorns.

"Shouldn't we wait for—" Peter began, but Corbin shushed him. It didn't feel right, the gate being left open like that. His suspicious mind questioned whether someone had wanted them to find it open like that.

And someone could be inside. *Lying in wait*.

"Stop being such a wanker," Corbin said as he followed the professor through the gate. "Even the bloody bookworm has more balls than you."

Peter leaned against the gate door, propping it open. He stared into a tunnel shrouded by thorns and shaped like a bullet standing on its end. He gripped his shovel, twisting it in his hands as if it were a chicken neck in need of wringing.

He stepped forward, then stopped and looked around for Merlin. He spotted the cat a few meters back, sitting on its haunches.

"You coming?"

The cat growled, low and guttural. It hissed and ran off.

Peter felt exposed and alone. His gut told him that he had another chance to turn back, that everything easy about the night's task had been too easy, too unlike all the other escapades he'd shared with Dervish. He felt as if he was being lulled into a false sense of security, and that scared him more than anything.

Fuck it. He marched through the gate.

A heavy, black blanket of air engulfed him. It smelled awful, like a hundred somethings had crawled in there to die. He covered his nose with his shirt. The intertwined branches of the roof formed a low arch. Here and there, pinholes of light broke through like stars on a painted ceiling. Cold, wet sand, somewhere between tan and mud, sifted into his shoes at his ankles. He couldn't see the others ahead of him—just an endless blackness leading down the gaping maw of night.

He reached for the walls in the hope he could use them to guide him along and immediately regretted it. Blood warmed his left hand where he'd pierced it against an unseen point. Thorns scratched at his right. He dropped the shovel. It slid into the branch barricade.

A concealed critter scurried away from him. He froze, hoping it had just been a crab but imagining a fleshy tail, red rat eyes, and overbiting teeth.

He fumbled blindly, his hands and arms poked and prodded worse than cattle driven to slaughter, until he found the shovel's handle jutting into the path about waist high. He pulled and found it stuck, so he gave it a hard yank. It came free quickly, and Peter stumbled backward into the opposite wall.

He immediately wished he'd worn his thick leather jacket. The yelp that escaped him was like that of a dog whose paw had been trampled. He eased forward, wincing from many points of pain spread wide across his back and neck.

"Hey, Dervish," Corbin said between chuckles. "I think Peter's scared of the dark."

Peter huffed. He flipped Corbin the bird, not that anyone could see it.

"Shut up, and keep moving." Dervish's voice was barely audible, coming from someplace way ahead and…

Down? After a few more steps, the decline steepened. His foot caught in the sand and he staggered, only to be rewarded with some more puncture wounds in his arm as he braced himself against the wall. He tore himself free, muttering obscenities like Yosemite Sam falling down a stairwell. His eyes finally began to adjust. With each step, his vision improved. The walls beside him revealed their contorted form, miniature crabs lumbering across the growth. Spider webs filled the spaces in the rutted barrier, their owners noticeably absent.

Something bit his shin, and he swatted at it madly. He couldn't see the midges, but he sure as shit could feel them. He thought he'd found their breeding ground on that cursed island. The air itself seemed aflutter. He hissed and scratched himself all over, dreaming of a vacation from his vacation.

Hell is infested with biting midges.

Not quite satisfied but as close as he figured he was going to be, Peter stopped scratching himself raw and noticed he was alone. He could no longer hear Corbin plodding in front of him. He wondered if the path had forked or worse, had forked more than once. He cursed his bad luck and power-walked, he hoped, to catch up with the group, not daring a jog on account that visibility still royally sucked. He nearly collided with Corbin before he caught site of the shorter man's graying ponytail. When he made out the rest of his old acquaintance, never a friend, he had to laugh. In the tight quarters, Corbin had resorted to a bow-legged duck waddle, the long duffel bag bouncing between his knees with each hurried half step. Sweat dampened the rim of his jeans.

Over Corbin's shoulder, a patch of light came in and out of view with the in-tempo movements of those in front of him. It grew bigger and brighter, and when Corbin stepped out into the open air, he stepped out of the way of a cool, crisp breeze that smelled of beauty and power, harmony and discord, and all the magic of the sea. And underneath it, the dank, dead, and putrefying odor of the tunnel lingered on his clothes.

Above, the moon shined on, full and proud as if seeking credit for its tug-of-war victory over the tides. Around him were walls, high and lush with creeping vines, the precipices of airy cliffs overlooking moss-covered bluffs. Peter hadn't realized just how much he had descended. The inn, the tavern, the town itself, all lay somewhere civilization yet held sway.

Someplace that seemed far away.

The cliff walls formed a narrow horseshoe that cordoned off the secret enclave, opened only at the end where waves barreled into a stony surf. The narrow pathway continued ahead, no longer hidden behind fences or thickets, the only passage to the beach free from dunes and elephant-sized boulders.

Straight ahead but still at least a hundred meters away, a woman crouched facing the water. She was little more than a black silhouette against a navy canvas. Her hair whipped in the wind like a kite angry for being tethered.

"Peter!" The voice was quiet but urgent. Dervish glowered at him from behind a massive rock that jutted from the earth like the fingertip of a buried titan. The woman at the shore rose, her lithe figure as beautiful as that of the goddess Athena under Selene's pale glow. She cupped an object in her hands. It was too small for Peter to make out, a rock or shell perhaps, and it glimmered like mirrored glass. She began to wrap the object in a garment of some sort when Peter heard Dervish call to him again.

As the woman began to turn, Peter ran to hide behind the boulder with the rest of his companions. Professor McCoy, who was on lookout at the other side, shrugged. Dervish shook his head. Peter held his breath. They'd know soon enough if he'd been spotted, he figured.

They crouched low, hugging themselves to the smooth, damp stone, its shadow embracing them in return. The rock was as big as a house, certainly big enough to shelter them from unwanted detection. Peter slid down to a knee and felt mud cake onto his jeans. Steadying himself against the boulder, he leaned out to admire the beauty as she passed.

Instead, he noticed the tracks the four men had made between the opening in the thicket and their hiding spot behind the boulder. If the woman looked down, she would see those tracks. She would find them.

He wondered if he should preempt their discovery by exposing himself, by throwing himself upon the mercy of the goddess. Being exposed beside her couldn't be all that bad, he figured. But as he rose to follow his impulse, a firm hand latched on to his collar and held him in place.

The woman paused beside the tracks, but she did not turn to see where they led. Peter could only see one side of her face, enough to watch the corner of her mouth curl up into a smile. He recognized her: the barmaid who'd delivered the round of free drinks at the tavern earlier that night. She was even more striking now, her long hair floating like smoke in the wind. Garbed in what looked like a white sarong, maybe a toga, the woman dazzled brighter than the stars and sparkling sea themselves.

He wondered if she was the girl who had stolen Matt's heart. In less than a few minutes, she had stolen his. Her movements were surreal, as liquid as ocean waves. Peter couldn't help but think that maybe there was some truth to the legends, that this woman was something more than she appeared. All his reservations about the *sidhe*, the *sith*, or whatever hell else Dervish had called them were vanquished by the stir in his heart. He would have run to her, but that man-claw on his shoulder kept him grounded.

As quickly as the grip tightened around his

collarbone, the magic was gone. He blinked, and the woman was only a woman — as she'd always really been, he knew. There was nothing special about this island. He'd allowed himself to become caught up in the moment, a beautiful woman against a foreign landscape on a serenely perfect night. He'd nearly forgotten his danger, that creepy walk through dead brush, and the fact that the leader of their expedition's son, and the only one of them worth a damn, was missing. Shame hit him in the gut. He looked up at the cliff edge high above and wished he had stayed behind with Merlin.

The barmaid plunked a bundle on the dirt in front of her. It resembled a blanket formed into a bag and tied to a stick like the kind hobos used to carry their things in old cartoons, *sans* the stick. She unfolded what at first appeared to be a towel until it lay flat on the sand, sleeves without arms reaching outward: a plaid shirt, red and black checkered, and a man's shirt by the look of it, much too big for the woman.

Matt's shirt?

Peter swallowed hard. A black square, possibly a wallet, a belt, sneakers, and a pair of jeans that appeared to be shredded lay on the shirt next to the object the barmaid had been holding down at the beach.

She picked up the object and held it high as if she wanted the world to see it. Peter could see it much better now, a tennis ball-sized rock with more sides that any polygon he could remember from geometry. In the moon's light, it shimmered and changed color from black to brown to orange to white and back to black again, a continuous cycle. Shaped like raw obsidian, the rock was remarkable even in its uncut form. Peter guessed it was both rare and valuable. He considered whether it might be a diamond or some other precious gemstone, maybe one he'd never seen before. He thought of his debt and guessed at the gem's worth, wondering where it had come from.

Then, it was gone. The woman placed it back into her shirt bundle, balled everything up, and slung it over her shoulder. She stepped into the tunnel.

"Maybe I should follow her," Peter said, his interests no longer salacious.

Dervish spun him around. "In due time."

"What do you mean? She might be able to tell us what happened to Matt."

"First, we explore the beach. Then we find Matt." He let go of Peter's jacket.

Peter did not try to hide his disgust. Dervish had always been greedy, and he'd always been selfish. He'd even always been willing to sacrifice those around him for the slightest chance at a big score. That much didn't surprise Peter. It was half the reason he'd gotten out. It was only a matter of time before Dervish would have sacrificed him as well. His phantom toe served as a tingling reminder of that every damn day.

But now they were discussing the man's only son. Peter had always seen pride in Dervish when he talked about Matt. The boy seemed to be the only thing that made the man human. Had Peter been wrong about him all that time? He glared up at Dervish with disdain in his heart.

Dervish offered a dopey grin and shrugged as if to pull a Popeye, *I yam what I yam*. He picked up his dog carrier and headed toward the surf, keeping to the relative cover of the dunes and the rocks.

The professor and Corbin followed. Again, Peter was left bringing up the rear. He picked his shovel off the ground and considered going after the woman anyway, but decided against it. *Where's she going to go at half past three on this tiny island?* He chased after Dervish, if not for any other reason than his desire to bash in the man's head. He wondered if he could swing the shovel hard enough to make a dent in a skull so thick.

He quickly caught up to the professor, who was breathing heavy and lagging behind the others. Together, they walked the rest of the way to the beach.

Waves crashed against rock pillars protruding from the depths, their white foam remains fizzling like the head on draught beer. Wet sand became dark mud that squished and oozed. Stones and shells blotted the alcove. The surrounding cliffs reached deep into the water, partitioning the small beach from the rest of the island. Black kelp coursed over the higher portions of the boulders like veins filled with infected blood.

The tide was rolling in.

The four men stood along the water's edge, staring out to sea. The horizon was eerily dark and bare. Black clouds blotted out the stars. Lightning flashed way off in the distance, the thunder drowned by the ocean's roar.

The wind whistled over the dunes and whipped through Peter's hair. He brushed a few stray strands from his forehead and squinted, but there was nothing for him to see.

Corbin broke their silence. "What exactly are we looking for?"

Dervish didn't answer him. He continued to stare out over the water, his mouth hanging open. Holding his hat onto his head, McCoy sighed and turned away.

"Matt said they'd be here," Dervish snapped. "They're here… somewhere. We just have to find them. Did you think it was going to be easy? Someone would have found them long ago if that were the case, mates."

"The fae?" Peter walked over to Dervish and pushed him, not hard but hard enough to make a point. "Really? That's truly your end game here? I thought for sure it had to be treasure, an ancient artifact, some long lost temple, maybe something even sort of believable like a Celtic burial mound. But goddamn faeries—"

"It's both. Laugh all you want, but the faeries are real. Matt may be a lot of things, but he ain't no goddamn liar."

"So sayeth the King of Lies. Did you ever consider that maybe he'd gotten himself into some trouble? That he said what he had to say to get you out here? Or worse, that he said what he was *told* to say?"

"We have code words for times like that."

Peter slapped his thighs. "Don't you remember what happened in the Paris crypts? Maybe he forgot them! Maybe he panicked! Maybe whoever you pissed off this time would have hurt him if he strayed from the script. Maybe… maybe they already have!"

He pushed Dervish again. Dervish raised a fist.

Professor McCoy stepped between them. "Will you two imbeciles be quiet?" He placed his palm against each of their chests. "I hear something."

Peter listened. Aside from the waves and his own heated breaths, he didn't hear a thing, until... *There!* "What is that?"

No one answered, everyone intent on the sound. It reminded Peter of that annoying, rapid-fire, little girl laughter in Japanese cartoons where friendly monsters exploded from bubbles to drink soda with obnoxious brats or spit at monkeys or have some other equally strange purpose.

Hehehehehehehehehehehehehehehe.

On and on, a soft cooing emitted from an unseen maker like the muted ringing of a dinner bell.

It stopped. Peter tilted his head toward the water, trying to aim his ear in the direction he thought the sound had come from. It came again. It stopped again.

Peter was about to repeat his question when Corbin stole the words from his mouth. "What the hell is that? And where is it coming from?"

His eyes having failed to locate the source of the noise, Peter trusted in his ears to fulfill the task. The hum seemed to come from the direction of the water. Thinking back to his science class and something he'd learned about sound travelling through liquids, he stared at the waves even as the sound came again. Still, he saw nothing.

He checked the boulders jutting out of the sea. Black specks crawled over the sprawling seaweed veins. He wondered if they were capable of making that sound, like the dull buzz of cicadas or the chirping of crickets. The specks lumbered along slowly and drunkenly. Peter decided they weren't responsible.

The humming resumed, louder, resonating through the water, echoing against the rocks. Peter's mind raced for an explanation. *Sonar perhaps?* Then, the sound was gone.

But something else remained.

Something in the water, something alive.

It stood stationary despite the swells, not far in, where dying waves stretched flat and thin. A pale gray hue, it might have been the tip of a rock he'd previously overlooked, if not for that shrill chirp.

Are those... eyes?

The object—*no, a living thing*—moved toward them. It stopped only a meter or two closer. A head poked above water. Russian-doll eyes, all painted and plastic and peculiarly humanoid, gazed at the men from a teardrop-shaped head that came to a point at its top. Its mouth looked frozen in a mixture of glee and surprise, round and open, baring no teeth. Wings of softest white, unadulterated cotton emerged from behind the life form's back. They folded over like the ears of a floppy-eared rabbit, dripping brine and entangled with vegetation.

The creature stepped closer still, and its arms rose from the depths—long, sharp-elbowed, and spindly with hairy hands having far too few fingers to be human. When it rubbed its gangling hands together, it produced another piercing, girlish giggle that split the silence like a falcon's cry through open air.

Behind it, maybe three meters, another head

breached the surface. Another appeared off to Peter's left, then another, and another, until they were sprouting like cabbage everywhere he looked. Each of the heads, though nearly identical in appearance, varied in size. Some were no bigger than fists, while one was as big as a toddler in a dunce cap. He suppressed a chuckle when he thought how much they reminded him of his wife's—*ex-wife's*—garden gnomes who had fought valiantly but futilely against Peter and his faithful steed, John Deere.

But these gnomes can actually fight back, if they have any fight to them.

Only when he tried to speak did Peter realize his mouth was hanging open. "Are those," he stammered. "They can't be..."

"Still think I'm an idiot?" Dervish asked as he crept closer to the water's edge. He slowly lowered the crate to the sand and hid the snare pole behind his back.

Peter normally would have had a hundred smartass answers for Dervish, but at the moment, he could think of none. Judging by the size if the faeries—*yes, for real, honest-to-God, afore-not believed flying fucking faeries*—or at least the parts of them he could see, Peter guessed the cage was big enough to house three or four of them easily.

Professor McCoy approached the shore with his hat clutched in both hands, its rim stuffed in his mouth. His eyes were wide with excitement. When he reached Dervish, he would have continued straight past him had the big man not thrown out his arm, signaling him to stay back. For the first time in the short while Peter had known him, the professor appeared something other than mousy and reserved. The smartest one of them had gone stupid.

"Shouldn't we keep our distance?" Peter asked, shaking off the mystique. "If these things are what I think you think they are, might they... I can't believe I'm saying this... know magic or something?" Warmth rose in his cheeks, and he felt foolish. "You know what I mean. They might be dangerous."

That didn't sound so ridiculous, but maybe a bit cowardly. He was okay with that. *Brave men die well.* The creatures were completely unknown to each and every one of them. What parts of the legends were true, if any? How could they know they were safe?

He hung back, not taking any chances. Corbin held his position too, and Peter was surprised to see the loose cannon exercising the most restraint. Peter had no clue what he should do. He decided to do nothing.

The *faery* (and Peter was still loathe to use the word aloud), the small sea person-thing, matched pace with Dervish, each taking slow, hesitant steps, tentative, perhaps afraid, though Peter had never known the man to fear anything. The wee man or woman, Peter sure as shit couldn't tell, should have been afraid. Greed oozed off Dervish like the Vaseline he used to slick down his mustache. That rare, unassuming, ignorant creature had no idea what evil lay inside that thug's heart. And that was assuming the faery-thing was intelligent life and not some dumb animal.

Peter knew. Looking at the faery's pure, soft features—its big, round eyes, wide and smiling, simple and guileless on smooth, glistening skin—he didn't think he could let Dervish take it, not if it meant hurting it.

But the dumb thing kept walking right on out of the water and into its enemy's hands. It didn't flinch or so much as blink; Peter wasn't sure it had eyelids. Only two meters separated it from Dervish. His smile grew wider as the faery closed the gap. Its body, pale gray and much fatter than Peter had expected, was round like a pumpkin. He did think it made the faery look more adorable, an opinion Corbin would no doubt link to his Peter-likes-them-heavy theory if he dared to share it. This thing, however, was almost grotesque, a gorged beach ball bobbing on the water, ready to explode with the addition of even one more molecule of air. It was so fat that it had no neck. Impossibly thin legs, too thin to conceivably support a body of such girth had not Peter witnessed it himself, carried the faery onto the shore. It walked bowlegged, waddled really. A rectangular tail dragged behind it like a wedding gown with long tresses at the corners.

The faery didn't appear to be wearing clothes, though Peter assumed it must have been because he couldn't see its genitalia. *Maybe they don't have genitals?* Peter pulled himself from his reverie. *What the fuck do I know about faeries?*

He rubbed his eyes, still not entirely confident what he saw was real. It wouldn't have been the first time he'd been slipped a narcotic while with Dervish. He pinched himself, then rubbed his eyes again. When they refocused, he saw that the faery was closer.

All of them were closer.

Their bravest, or most foolhardy, was already within poking distance of Dervish. He crouched and waved the fingers of his upturned palm at the creature. "Come here, little bugger," he said soothingly as if coaxing a baby to walk. "Come to Papa." He smirked. "Come make Papa a rich son of a bitch."

The professor hung over his shoulder. Even Corbin's wariness seemed to have vanished as he leaned in closer to the garden gnome lookalike. Peter was sure he'd still throw any one of them to the wolves should things go badly.

Dervish laid the back of his hand on top of the sand. Goosebumps coursed over Peter's arms and neck as the faery walked right onto it. The trusting twit obviously lacked any brain power if it wasn't smart enough to be afraid. Dervish didn't prove to be much wiser; he had the rarest creature in all of antiquity, a living gold mine, perched complacently in his hand, but lacked the presence of mind to seize his opportunity. Peter wondered how long that would last.

The creature leaned forward, its two-toed feet testing Dervish's palm like a dog trying to find a perfect spot to lie. It swayed like a drunk reeling before a fall. The pose seemed awkward, as if the faery's legs were never meant to hold it upright, its fat torso too much for them to carry. It was going to fall. Peter was sure of it. And when it did, Dervish would have his prize.

The faery did fall, and as it tumbled, it curled its head into itself, Peter assumed to protect its face. The top of its head drove into Dervish's wrist.

Dervish howled.

McCoy jumped back. Corbin threw his hands up in defense.

"What?" Peter cried, only vaguely aware he was moving backward.

"The fucker stabbed me!" Dervish lashed out at the faery, now lying on its face in the sand.

*That's not its face...*Peter froze. Nothing was right about that creature. Nothing at all. Every fiber of Peter's body screamed caution, every nerve ending flashed warning. In the midst of his racing thoughts, a subliminal message repeated: *Run.*

Still, fear rooted his feet in the dirt. Dervish's face flushed red with rage. Blood trickled from his wrist. He growled as he dug from it a four-inch shaft, buried beneath his skin like a splinter.

Even in the terse period of tense silence that followed Dervish's rampage, Peter knew the creature was not what it had seemed. It surely was no faery. The face was not a face, but a stomach. *An abdomen.*

"Mimesis," the professor muttered. He kept his distance but that look of wonderment, of dangerous curiosity, lingered on his face.

Mimesis? Peter didn't know the word, but he knew "mime" and "mimic" and guessed the professor had seen what he was seeing: a sort of camouflage, something animals used to hide from or scare off predators.

Or to lure in prey.

Peter knew enough about the animal kingdom to know that camouflage was fairly common. Chameleons, those long stick insects, and the other kind that looked like leaves, even butterflies that looked like their poisonous cousins, all had an extra level of protection grounded in deception.

Then there were the spiders with coloring that matched their favorite floral hangouts, yellow or white exoskeletons on matching petals. This deception helped them hunt. It helped them kill. Peter had even heard of a mantis whose entire body looked like a wild orchid. All it had to do was sit still, and food would land in its mouth.

"Goddamn it!" he shouted. Other than what had happened to Dervish, who'd been holding one, the creatures had shown no aggression. He wondered if they were truly dangerous, but he did not want to stick around to find out. "I knew there was no such fucking thing as fucking goddamn faeries. Be careful!"

"Grab it, Dervish," Corbin said. "Faery or not, I bet that thing's worth something. A new discovery."

Dervish did more than grab it. As his mammoth boot came down on the creature, crunching and pulverizing the unknown species into the sand, Peter saw it for what it was. Two legs separated and became four. The faux faery arms, with knobby joints and cilia covered hands, were another set of legs with needle-nose pliers for feet. The creature's wings were not wings, but a fourth set of legs oddly curled and lathered with a soapy-stringy secretion. Its face was also false, a mere pattern on skin, a tattooed facsimile with the sole purpose of diverting its on-looker's attention from the sinister truth at its opposite end.

The wedding gown.
The head.
Four rows, each with a half-dozen eyes, red and

bulging like blistering skin, lined the top of a squared head. What Peter had thought were tassels or tresses were the two prongs of a zigzagging mandible.

A crab? Not quite, at least not one he'd ever want to eat. The false wings had given the creature away, though he didn't want to believe what his mind told him it was, that arachnids could grow so big. Even the goliaths he'd seen down in Brazil weren't nearly that big, and they were mostly docile. These were the size of cocker spaniels.

And then it was broken, crunching like flattened potato chips, a splintered pile of exoskeleton and yellow bile. Dervish ground his heel into the dying beast as it emitted a cry that sounded like a teakettle whistle. It twitched twice before giving up the fight.

Dervish lifted his foot and held it aloft in front of him. Webbing wrapped his boot's toe. A line of goop ran from his heel onto the sand like snot from a toddler's nose. He swayed, and his arms went out for balance, but he did not fall. He swiped the back of his hand across his forehead. It came off wet.

The flesh on his wrist curdled and died. "Some kind of poison," he said as he raised it for the others to see.

"Suck it out," Peter said. His voice shook. He looked at his hands and saw that they were shaking, too.

"No," Professor McCoy said, grabbing Dervish's arm as he raised his mutilated wrist to his mouth. "You'll only succeed in spreading the decay to your face. We need to slow the spread of it through your veins, place a tourniquet just below the elbow—"

That mad hyena giggle erupted from the ocean

floor. The creatures were rubbing their legs together in unison. They stopped and disappeared under the surface.

Then they came ashore.

"Corbin," Dervish called. "Help me catch one."

"Fuck that," Corbin replied. He turned and ran.

"Forget them," Peter said. "It's not worth it." Two creatures had emerged from the water. One bent its pipe cleaner legs and launched itself into the air. Its jaw snapped open and closed as it soared straight at Peter's chest.

Peter raised the shovel and swung. He almost smiled as he connected, sending the wicked beast back into the ocean. "We have to go!" But when he glanced to his left, he saw it was too late. The professor was on the ground, screaming as three of the creatures crawled atop him and stung him with poison-filled stingers. They struck him like pissed-off wasps with piston-like blades drilling for oil. His fedora lay discarded in the surf.

Dervish strangled one ugly critter in his hands, crushing it as easily as a tomato while another crawled up his pant leg. He was all rage and no caution, too blinded by bloodlust to recognize his peril.

Peter had been too preoccupied with the others' problems to recognize his own. He glanced back to the ocean in time to see two more of the spidery monsters come ashore, but where was the third he'd seen? He heard a chirping sound at his feet and looked down to see the creature, its abdomen curling like a scorpion raising its tail to strike. His body reacted. He drove the shovel down just as the arachnid went for the kill.

The stinger hit the shovel with a dull clang.

The shovel severed the creature in half.

Shots rang to his left. Dervish, still on his feet, was picking off the creatures one by one with the aim of seasoned marksman. A horde of dead and dying piled up around him.

Still, the monstrosities came.

"Come on, Dervish," Peter yelled. He turned to run, tripped over a stone, and fell onto the sand.

He struggled to regain his feet, but something hit him hard in the back. He rolled forward, laid prone on his back. A creature rolled like tumbleweed away from him.

It rose and pounced onto Peter's chest.

He yelped and grabbed at the creature's front legs, holding it back as its jaws snapped and slashed over his face. Hot fluid sprayed from its mouth, sizzling on Peter's skin.

The thing was strong, its body as heavy as a big dog. Only its legs seemed to be weak points, skinny spiny shafts like thin branches at the top of a great tree. Peter pulled the forelegs in opposite directions, earning a satisfying crack.

The spider rolled off him, squealing and sputtering curses in an inhuman tongue. Peter scrambled for the tunnel, his heart beating feverishly.

I have to get to the gate. I have to get out.

Halfway across the dead expanse of rocks and dunes, he ran into Corbin.

And the wall of humans holding him at gunpoint.

Peter recognized a few of them: the barmaid, the bartender, the hotel clerk, even the cheery, cheeky bastard who had escorted him to the island. They all wore the same garb, that white toga-like get up. For the second time that night, the barmaid gave him a wink.

"You see," the bartender said, "we've struck a bargain of sorts with the slaugh."

"What?" Peter's heart thumped in its cage. Corbin stared at him with terror in his eyes and brow raised as if to ask, "What are we going to do?" Peter wished he had an answer.

The bartender grinned like a used car salesman that had just sold them a lemon. "We give them you, and they give us your belongings—"

"You'd kill us for a few bucks and some credit cards—"

The bartender laughed. "No, no. We wouldn't be stupid enough to use your credit cards. If one of us did, he or she would share your fate. We're well compensated for our efforts, but that's no concern of yours."

Peter remembered what the barmaid had been carrying, that hard-edged gem that shimmered like mirrored glass. *Just how valuable is it?* He shuddered. *Was it her reward for giving them Matt?*

"March yourself back down to that beach." The bartender aimed his shotgun at Peter's face. "Do it now, and I won't have to shoot you."

"Shoot us?" Corbin's laugh was nervous and wild. He turned to Peter. "Don't you see? For whatever reason, they want us alive. He won't shoot us. Run! He's not gonna shoot—"

A deafening blast sent Peter's world into chaos. Corbin had taken only a single step when a huge chunk of his thigh disintegrated. He fell to the ground, writhing in pain, screaming in agony.

His wails were muffled. Time seemed to slow. "Alive, yes." The bartender chuckled. "But nobody said you had to be in one piece." He walked over to Corbin. "You shouldn't have done that. The slaugh will have to find another use for you now."

The words snapped Peter from his shock. Any fate these terrible people could throw his way had to be better than what awaited him at the shore. Running seemed the only choice.

He juked to his left, only to find the beautiful barmaid pointing a pistol at his face. Peter stopped in his tracks.

"You... you... you fucker," the injured Corbin seethed between moans. He arched his back, quickly slipping a hand underneath.

The gun. Peter waited for his opening.

The bartender didn't see it coming. Corbin pulled the gun and fired. He screamed as he unloaded six bullets into the bartender's chest, squeezing the trigger even after the bartender collapsed.

The night fell silent, except for the *click click click* of the revolver. The townsfolk seemed shocked, their eyes transfixed on the two figures bleeding into the sand.

Peter saw his chance.

He leapt into action. The barmaid toppled easily as he pushed her aside. He drove his shoulder into one of the townsfolk, the drunken old man from the lounge, plowed through him and kept on running. If they shot him in the back, he figured so what? Death seemed frightfully better than being offered to the...

What had he called them? The slaugh?
Fuck the slaugh.

He ran as fast as he was able, the sound of pursuit never far behind him. The townsfolk shouted as he made his way into the tunnel, their curses echoing through the passage. Darkness swallowed him. Branches snagged on his clothes. Thorns stabbed his face.

Still, he ran on.

The door! I have to make it through the door, find some place to hide. Or a boat! Anything that will get me off this fucking island.

He collided with the door in the dark. Momentarily dazed, he shook the stars out of his eyes and pushed. The hinges creaked slightly, but the door did not budge.

"No. No. No. No!" He punched the gate so hard, the skin on his knuckles split. Peter peeked through the cracks and saw a boy with dark hair who he recognized: the boy who had bumped into him at the hotel.

"You!" A glimmer of hope made him delirious. "Open the door," he begged. "Please. Open the door."

"I warned you," the boy said. "I told you to leave while you still could. It's too late now."

The boy walked away. Merlin trotted beside him.

"No... wait... I—"

Something slammed into the back of his head.

He fell to the ground.

***

A CLEAR VIEW of a darkening sky greeted Peter as

he awoke. Black clouds swallowed the last embers of starlight. Lightning crackled. Droplets pitter-pattered on his cheeks. They were cool, refreshing.

Dreamlike.

Peter wanted to believe it had all been a dream. In his semi-groggy, awakening state, he could almost fool himself.

Until he tried to move.

The edge of a wave licked at his feet. A shot of icy cold jolted through his body. He shivered violently, but couldn't move his arms, his legs, not even a finger or toe. He was paralyzed.

No! He strained, struggled, concentrated all his focus on his left hand. It was no use. He couldn't raise it, couldn't even be sure it was still there.

He tried to scream, but only a whine came out, bringing with it gurgling drool. He felt spit slide down his jaw. He *felt* it. *If I am paralyzed, why can I still feel?*

Another wave tickled his heel, and he froze all over again. His eyes—he could move them. A splash came from his left. He sensed movement in his peripheral. Something big and white, pill-shaped, like a coffin, slid toward the water.

His body tingled as goosebumps formed on his flesh. *Like that feeling you get when a spider crawls across it.* The thought made him queasy. Still, he hadn't seen the creatures, and he prayed he wouldn't.

He was cold, so very cold. He inspected himself as his immobility would permit. His chest was bare. So were his toes. What had happened to his shirt and shoes? He had to assume everything in between was naked, too. He felt humiliated, defiled.

A sudden electric buzz rose into the night, and he knew the creatures were near. His heart thudded in his chest as he screamed inside his mind, unable to do a damn thing.

A pale devil lumbered onto his chest. Its pointed feet prodded him, and he felt as if he was being jabbed with a fork. A thick strand of white nastiness that resembled string cheese trailed along behind the creature. The abomination reeked like an infected cyst.

Another joined it, crawling over his legs. They worked the thread into a thin, stretchy mesh. They were wrapping him, preparing him for dinner—to be externally digested and slurped up like soup, no doubt.

The creatures made several passes over his body. When they first passed over his face, he thought his heart would stop. He closed his eyes and wished it would. The revolting secretions encircled his head like mummy wrappings. The pungent goo burned like salt on his lips.

He felt as though he had been tucked firmly into bed. After a few minutes of silence, he felt himself moving. Frigid cold water lapped at his calves as the creatures pulled him into the ocean. The cocoon kept him dry, but provided no warmth.

His body bobbed across the waves. He felt a tugging at his feet, felt himself being pulled under. The sounds of the surface vanished. His ears popped. His teeth chattered. The cold became unbearable. He continued to sink. He didn't know how fast or for how long, only that it was getting colder, quieter, emptier. In the silence, he was sure he would soon lose his grasp on sanity. He began to wonder why he fought to keep it. The air in his tomb was running out. Breathing became a chore. His lungs burned.

He decided to relax and let go.

Suffocating wasn't as peaceful as he'd hoped. He gasped. The air inside his cocoon was gone. His eyes bulged, trying to climb from their sockets. Peter wanted to claw at his throat, open up the airway, but he was unable to move.

Wait... I did move! It was only a finger, but Peter was sure he'd straightened it. He tried again. Yes, he was certain. His fingers were bending to his will, but he lacked the strength to tear through the wrappings.

Where will I find myself if I claw my way out?

His mind fluttered between sleep and consciousness, his bouts of the latter coming less and less frequent. He heard a noise: muffled screaming. It grew louder. With a splash, oxygen returned, and he sucked it in with long, pained draws.

Sounds came rushing in with the air. They came from everywhere around him: skittering, banging, shouting, screaming—it was as if he'd be dragged into the center of a battlefield. The sounds grew louder, and he stopped moving. He felt a cold, hard slab of earth beneath him.

Peter listened, anxious, unable to imagine what was happening outside his white sarcophagus. He couldn't handle another shock. He just wanted to lie there and be still, alone and untouched until he withered away.

He heard a rip, like box cutters through packaging tape. It came again and again, fabric tearing in long swaths. An eerie glow, shifting from blue to green to orange and back again, became more vibrant each time he heard the sound. *Some discoveries are better left unmade.*

Large shadows moved over him. A sharp pain shot through his stomach and he groaned. *The fuckers stung me!* He wondered how many times he'd already been stung, how black and dead his flesh had become.

He caught sight of a knife as it oscillated up and down, drawing nearer to his face.

It was cutting him free.

The sounds of human suffering forced their way through the opening into his cocoon. He wanted to block his ears, didn't want those terrible noises entering his snug hideaway. He didn't want to see the outside world, content to spend eternity in that mass of webs if it meant he'd never have to see what was coming for him.

A faint light washed over him as the wrappings parted. He raised an arm as he squinted at the shadow standing over him, masked by an eerie glow. Photosynthetic critters in the shallow pools around him, disturbed by movement, lit up in brilliant blue and green streaks of bioluminescence.

A subterranean cavern spread out in all directions around him; cathedral-like ceilings loomed high above. The walls flittered with life: fireflies glowed orange and yellow. The bugs reminded Peter of Tinkerbell. *Of fucking faeries!* His lip quivered at the irony.

Pillar-sized stalagmites rose from the floor. Stalactites hung from the ceiling like pointed teeth in a monstrous mouth. He stared at his outstretched hand. *I moved my arm!* It was enough to spawn a glimmer of hope. His eyes focused on the hand that held the knife that freed him—a *human* hand. His gaze followed the arm up to its owner, a familiar face, one that was very much alive.

"Matt?" Peter blinked. The face of a boy he once knew still showed within the lines of a man. His father's jaw and steely eyes could not be mistaken. "Matt? Matt! Oh God, it is you, isn't it? You're alive!"

Dervish's own flesh and blood had freed him from certain damnation. Peter wept, tears of joy, tears of hope. He managed to sit up and filled with elation.

Until he looked around and heard the screams, and all hope died.

The screams came from Corbin. Sand and pebbles coated the cavity that the gunshot had blasted in his thigh, a bowl of shredded meat and tendon. His face had gone milk white from fear or blood loss, his clothes torn off and cast aside. Two spidery beasts, each as big as a wolverine, hauled him by his ankles, their web strands, thick as rope, squeezing tighter into his skin with each heave. They were pulling him toward a pit where—*For the love of God!*—their hungry young waited.

Corbin turned to his stomach, digging his fingers into the mud as he searched for ruts in the cavern floor. His hands briefly found a hold, but the creatures yanked him free without breaking stride.

The sea spiders detached their lines.

Corbin fell into the pit.

The echoes of his screams outlasted the man. After a few minutes, Corbin was barely more than a head and collar bone.

"We need to get out of here!" Peter blurted, his attention returning to Matt. "Please! Help me up!" He reached for Matt's hand.

Matt didn't give it. "Matt! Help me up. We need to go. Now!"

Peter pleaded, but Matt didn't move. "What's wrong? Why won't you help me?" The young man just stood there, brain dead like a zombie, his expression flat and unmoving. Except for some kind of hat, with straps that crisscrossed his face, Matt was naked. He'd been stung at least four times: once in each leg, a third to the left of his stomach, and the fourth in his neck. Fluid dribbled from the center of each.

After a moment spent with Matt doing nothing and Peter unable to rise, the young man tilted his head like a dog listening to a sound only it could hear. His strange hat twitched. The thin, straw-like straps that crossed his brow, the bridge of his nose, and above and below his lips opened in succession and closed again, tightening around the skin. Matt didn't seem to mind them. Peter wondered if he even knew where he was. The boy appeared to be an empty shell.

A vessel.

Peter swallowed hard, realizing that what he'd mistaken for straps were in fact legs. The rest of the creature was affixed to the back of Matt's head and neck. *For what purpose?*

He scooted back on his buttocks, trying to stand but his legs remained useless. A *chirp chirp chirp* erupted from his right. Peter turned to stare into mandibles the size of tree pruners. Hot spittle showered down on him. He closed his eyes, preparing for the end.

But the creature merely stepped over him, one pair of celery stalk legs followed by the next. Pete thought it was toying with him, that at any moment, it would stop and rip out his guts, jab him repeatedly with its samurai-sword stinger, but it kept walking.

Toward Dervish.

Torn flesh hung off the hulking man like melted cheese. He'd been punctured multiple times, pumped so full of poison he'd piss it out. Still, he fought on with nothing but the weapons he'd been gifted at birth, fists the size of mallets. Peter knew Dervish was tough, but glistening with sweat, clawed, stabbed, and coated with the blood and guts of his enemies, his former partner seemed invincible.

And maybe his only chance to escape.

Broken and mutilated bodies littered the cavern floor. Several of the spider monsters—it was impossible to total the number dead given they had been ripped to pieces—lay at Dervish's massive feet. Madness brimmed in his manic eyes.

The creatures retreated, conceding defeat. They sent their slaves to fight in their stead. Humans rose from shadowy corners, each with their puppet masters tapped into their craniums. A woman with luminescent skin and a mat of dingy red hair lunged at Dervish. A cluster of other humans trailed her like a pack of wolves. Their spider co-pilots chirped. En masse, they charged.

Dervish grabbed the red-headed woman by her scrawny neck and tore her away from him. He drove her head upward, impaling it on a stalactite. He punched another person so hard that Peter saw his jaw dislodge. Dervish broke his next attacker's back over his knee.

Matt's head rose, like a robot being activated. He turned toward his father and charged, latching onto his arm. Several more rushed behind him, smothering Dervish. In that group, Peter saw Professor McCoy, his entire intellect reduced and subjugated.

Dervish fell. Peter recoiled as the human horde pinned his only remaining ally to the ground. The largest spider, big as a black bear, moved atop its squirming and defiant victim. Dervish roared as the spider eased its stinger into his pelvis as if it were making love to him, pumping him full of death.

The king of the beasts stepped away. The human puppets sat Dervish up, his eyelids fluttering.

"Wake up!" Peter shouted. "Wake up, damn it!"

A sea spider crawled up Dervish's back. A thin needle slid into the base of his skull as the creature's legs connected over his face.

Dervish stood. He turned toward Peter, staring with the same lifeless eyes as his son. In fact, all the humans were staring at him that way.

A sea spider leaped onto his lap. In each of its bulging red eyes, Peter saw scorn.

Evil.

Peter thrashed as the malevolent life form clambered around him, but his movements were slow, drugged. The creature easily avoided his efforts. He felt it climbing up his back, creeping higher and higher.

Searing heat pierced tender flesh just above the nape of his neck. A haze clouded his mind. As if in a dream, he watched himself rise. His feet, no longer under his control, carried him past the pit of plump little ones, through twists and turns, over obstructions and along narrow ridges, to a place that glimmered like mirrored glass. Its surface reflected a gargantuan cavern, as big as an amphitheater, draped with stalactites and stalagmites, with precious gems and ores, with spider parasites and their human hosts, hundreds of both, all mining with chisels in hand.

And digging.

Expanding their underground world.

***

ACKNOWLEDGMENTS

The author would like to thank Scarlet Áingeal for her beta read services and knowledge of all things Scotland; Evans Light for his samurai editing skills; and Mike Tenebrae for his insane artistic talents. The author would also like to thank Kimberly Yerina, Erin Sweet-Al Mehairi, Abigail Grace, Robert Dias, Adam Light, Ken Parent, Victoria Parent, Elsie Parent, Frank Spinney, Jody Raymond, Alicia Rosen and all his friends and family for the support they've shown this and his work in general. This one is for all of you!

Jason Parent
Author of WHAT HIDES WITHIN and SEEING EVIL

About the Author

In his head, JASON PARENT lives in many places, but in the real world, he calls New England his home. The region offers an abundance of settings for his writing and many wonderful places in which to write them. He currently resides in Southeastern Massachusetts with his cuddly corgi named Calypso. He is the author of the novels SEEING EVIL, WHAT HIDES WITHIN and many published short stories.

Connect Online:

authorjasonparent.com

www.facebook.com/AuthorJasonParent

Made in the USA
Middletown, DE
28 February 2016